For Tanya, who was full of light – D.C.

Shine Moon Shine

First published in hardback in 2007
This paperback edition first published in 2008
by Hodder Children's Books

Text copyright © David Conway 2007
Illustrations copyright © Dubravka Kolanovic 2007

Hodder Children's Books
338 Euston Road
London NW1 3BH

Hodder Children's Books Australia
Level 17/207 Kent Street
Sydney, NSW 2000

ISBN 978 0 340 930847

Printed in China

Hodder Children's Books is a
division of Hachette Children's Books.
An Hachette Livre UK Company.
www.hachettelivre.co.uk

WRITTEN BY
DAVID
CONWAY

Shine
Moon
Shine

ILLUSTRATED BY
DUBRAVKA
KOLANOVIC

Hodder
Children's
Books

A division of Hachette Children's Books

ONE
SNOWY NIGHT
IN A GREAT BIG CITY

the moon fell from the sky and landed

on top of a very tall building. All the people

in the neighbourhood tried to put the moon

back into the night sky, but every

time they tried the moon

fell again.

That night a young boy
named Ata sat with the moon
to keep it company.

The moon warmed towards Ata for his kindness
and told him why it had fallen out of the night
sky and why it did not want to return.

"It is so dark up there,"
the moon told Ata. "It makes me feel so lonely."

Ata wanted to help the moon so the following morning he got up early and captured sunbeams in a bucket. And that night he carried them to the very tall building.

Ata climbed the stairs higher and higher and, when he reached the very top, where the moon sat pale and pensive, he released the sunbeams into the inky sky.

When this was done the dark night didn't look so dark anymore.

But the sunbeams didn't stay and as quickly as they had appeared they melted away.

The next day
Ata found a box
of old torches and
carried them to
the very tall
building.

Again Ata climbed the stairs higher and higher and, when he reached the very top, Ata filled the night with beacons of light.

When this was done the dark
night didn't look so dark anymore.

But the beacons of light
began to wane
and slowly
grew dimmer.

Then one by one they all went out.

On the third day Ata found
a ladder and carried this to the very
tall building.

Once again
Ata climbed the
stairs higher and
higher. When he reached
the very top Ata pushed
his hands through the
cold dark night and
made holes to let
the daylight in.

But the
holes in the
tender night
didn't stay and
slowly began to
close until the
sky was very
dark again.

Ata sat in
the roof's cold snow,
sad that the night would
not have a moon and sad
that the moon would never
have a home.

As the tears fell from
his eyes and landed on
the soft white snow they
became cold, so cold
that they began
to freeze.

When Ata noticed this he stopped
crying and picked up one of his frozen tears.
As it glistened in the darkness he had an idea.

Ata gathered up his frozen tears from the soft white snow

and threw them far and wide into the inky sky.

"If you go back home now," said Ata to the moon,

"you will never be lonely again."

The moon trusted Ata and slowly
but surely sailed away up into the darkness.

Then Ata cried at the top of his voice,

"Shine Moon Shine."

As Ata said this, the moon's bright beams poured into the frozen tears, filling them with such rich moonlight

that they lit up the night in a spectacular display.

All of the people in the neighbourhood cheered
and sang and clapped and danced as the moon
illuminated a new night sky.

For now the night didn't look so dark anymore,
and thanks to Ata and his frozen tears...

...the moon was never lonely again.

Other great Hodder picture books perfect to share with children:

978 0 340 89329 6

978 0 340 91161 7

978 0 340 91779 4

978 0 340 91153 2

978 0 340 93241 4 (HB)

Hodder
Children's
Books

A division of Hachette Children's Books